YOUNG POEMS

THE PATH

BARBARA CASTELNUOVO

PREFACE

Only those who love know. Only those who can go beyond the boundaries of rationalization and follow instinct, running through the grasslands of the senses ... Only those who love are alive. Blessed is he who loves.

POEMS

TO MY DAUGHTER

It is not a wish, love, but a solemn oath
so that you can have a lived childhood;
wonderful memories to fill your suitcase with
that you will take yourself into your world of woman;
rainy days to meditate to blossom
sunflowers in the heart, at the first hint of light.
I want to fill the deep pockets of your heart
using love, magic, and small pearls of wisdom
that I humbly collected from my experience.
I want to tell you about your immeasurable value

so that you can love yourself even in solitude
avoiding having to settle for an empty presence
by your side, having the patience to wait
your slice of paradise on which you can
unroll your love dreams and lie on them.
I want you never to look for my hand
for you will always find it enclosed on yours;
and that your footsteps on the world always find
an awareness, a profound sense;
that you can always marvel at the thousand shades
that color the world, and can cultivate your dreams
on fertile soils, with the complicity of the moon.
I want you to know pity
without ever seeing the face of cruelty
and love the sound of peace without having to hear
the silences of death, which are cruel echoes of unnecessary wars.
Finally, I want you to know that if you offer the good
you will not always be repaid in the same way
but alone you will understand that in the long run the good always pays.
Even if only in the quiet of your consciousness.
Know that the ones I want for you, my baby,
are the rights of all children in the world.
Rights that are often stolen.
Never forget to return what you received as a gift
because love must be handed down.
Only in this way will the world be enriched, with the hope that
one day no one feels the need to hate.

TO MY FATHER

The words
that I've never told to you
my father
I am the book
that I read every day
in my heart
since you
live there
where the pines
aim the sky
and talk to the sun.

TO MIRKO

Looking in the night darkness,
I can see billions of bright stars
in which I see the features of your delicate face.
And hearing the noises of the night
I can hear the echo of a stream
reminiscent of your melodious voice.
Asleep, I live a fantastic dream
and I wake up in the light of a splendid sunrise
full of confidence and serenity
because now you are with me,
in front of my eyes
that you smile at me and look at me
as never before I had hoped
and not even dreamed ...

◆ ◆ ◆

TO A FRIEND

The shadow of the trees
inside the solemn river
how mist melts,
in the meantime
Nightingales complain
among the tall branches.

How much, o friend
this landscape
he mirrored me,
how sad they cried
on top of the real leaves
hopes now drowned!
I see you again
I close my eyes slowly
neighbors we laughed together.
I was laughing too
through my tears.
Of course they will remain among all
those moments
like the most painful
but also the most beautiful.

◆ ◆ ◆

GOODBYE TO THE MOUNTAINS

Goodbye
green mountains
that you accompanied me
in dreams
in desires,
where the sun was strong
and burning despondency.
Goodbye

small countries
in the fresh air
to my lost soul
and blue sky
trees, rivers, paths ...
Goodbye
Sweet mountains ...

◆ ◆ ◆

IN THE SUN

There he is
The sun
He turns to me
His eyes,
source of life and hope
shine on us.
High in the sky
Beautiful sun
Warm up and give courage.
Light up my land.
You did not wake from sleep
The thankless rain.
Your grace

it is complete happiness,
to be there
to give hope
now lost.

◆ ◆ ◆

SUNRISE

This night
I dreamed of a world
where peace reigned.
But then the dawn
took away
everything with you
and left me
just a sad memory
for the room.

BROTHERLY LOVE

It is the dawn of life
the birth
that sees us innocent
and full of love
towards each other.
The hours of the day
then adolescence
and maturity
there are pitfalls
that can make an enemy
who was friend,
foreigner
who loved each other as a brother.
The hours of the day
they can take you far.
We have to learn
to love us
before night falls,
know
and understand each other
like brothers.

ANDROMEDA

You won't bend over
to the fury of the sea
trust is in you.
It is the weak point
that shows
also your strength,
the heart
so noble
to be able to forgive
but strong
to rebel against fate.

AUTUMN

In melancholy
of this Padan autumn
I walk alone
almost held back by the wet leaves
that invite me
to listen
the sacred hymns
that brings the wind
through the toneless air.
in the meantime
dart the sun
with a monotonous beam
on the lawn all yellow.
I walked
inside the small garden
gently lit.
from the morning sun
that sows every flower
of an opaque light.
This autumn
cradle with sweet songs
our heart
who forgets,

while strange fantasies
they parade around me
and accompany me
in the restless wind
that brings me here
and beyond
like a dead leaf.

BLACK CHILDREN

Empty eyes
off,
in black children
who play,
astonished
in this penumbra
than our hearts
impregnates.

I THINK

I believe in the words you whispered to me.
I believe in your perfume.
I experienced the unexpected taste of your mouth.
You are now beyond sunset,
beyond that subtle border,
even a cloud could hide you.
And it is there at the bottom
that I'm going to look for you in my nights.
I listen to the air around me,
I listen to your eyes and your hands.
Your voice is the softest sound of the night....
The air around me
change color every time I think of you,
vibrate on the calm waves of my body,
expanding towards me,
embraces me and leaves me enchanted,
loose and light. ...

SINCE WHEN

Ever since I fell in love with you, every look,
every smile, every thought,
every moment of my life are deeply tied to your heart,
You brought infinite wealth into my life. A little
of your love is enough to fill my life.
The world is big, the universe is huge,
but nothing is bigger and more sincere than my love for you.
Love me as long as you want, because in love there is life
and I want yours with me to be infinite.
Love me as I love you for no reason.

GODDESS ATHENA

Warm with light
the seed
in me it sprouts,
from ice
on fire
my heart sets.
Long strength
my mind refreshes
eternal goddess
my arm
not tired.

❖ ❖ ❖

DESIRE

I immolated my soul
on the altar of your desire,
weak the flesh to offer delight to temptation.
Strands of light embroider the shadows,
and a light sweat on the skin.
Instinct has the upper hand
on reason and impulse
of a magical moment.
A smile, a hug
and the breath is already short
breathless belly beats
to the heat of a quivering idea.
The desire escapes from the prison of hesitations,
he loses control to follow in his footsteps
of your bold hand.

Devour my thoughts with your mouth
Wound my skin, they are brush strokes
who paint a canvas in color
that passion alone enchants.
And then the wind rises
that comes suddenly
and not to escape.
I arch
and of my taste your face smells you.

You are mine, you are mine
between my feathers of gentle caresses.
The night is inflamed
you crossed my borders
it is a pleasure that travels,
melody of sighs.

You smelled my smell
and the desire for love assails you.
Tear off my clothes
discover the hidden acacia wood.

The day closing its wings
in the dark it disappears.
It's cold around now,
the bivouac lights up
and a free embrace
in the black silence.
Cover my body by swaying.
Velvet caresses velvet.
Manly contact invades me.

Lion
now taste the prey.
Exhausted we give our breaths to the moon.
This is the last moment.

WHERE THE DAY ENDS

I would like to meet you
where the day ends,
undress us from doubts and fears,
unite our bodies
in one dance,
let us discover lovers from the night ...

The deep look of your eyes
the intoxicating smell of your skin
the strength of your forms
the fresh tone of your voice ...
everything makes me vibrate,
everything makes me want to be yours ...

TWO DIFFERENT LOVES

How many stars tonight overlooking a dream
someone leans over and falls into the sea
a desire looks at her but cannot speak to her
It is something immense that cannot be explained
I never believed in fairy tales
..but one with you, however, I lived it
it lasted a second
but it is the most beautiful in the world
Nothing deeper has ever existed
of what now binds us forever
in our corner of light in the dark of the world
An infinite joy exploded in my life
an unrepeatable emotion a delicious sensation
My lips will retain the flavor forever
of that magical moment that made my heart tremble
The strongest feeling that has ever been experienced
a reality more beautiful than what has ever been dreamed
An indefinable ... indelible emotion ...
Now we are close every night like two bright stars
during the day your perfume caresses my skin
Your radiant smile makes my eyes shine

like the moon at night which is reflected in the sea
Our destinies fly parallel
towards infinity they have only certainty
of an immense feeling of infinite purity
two parallel destinies distant a caress
At night I'm afraid that everything ends
but then in the morning like a flower it is reborn
It is the strongest feeling that has ever been experienced
a reality more beautiful than what has ever been dreamed
An emotion created only for us
A special emotion that never ends ...

UNTIL THE MORNING WILL COME

Caress my hips
with your secret dreams,
guard my heart,
tying my thoughts ...
I will make you fly,
if you really want it,
I will be your wishes
I'll take your breath away ...
You can voice silence
of your fantasy
and give her my name,
like a melody
soaked between the lips.
You will distill the perfume
that veils my skin
drawing with your fingers
chills on my shoulders.

You will have my sweetness
as a secret brand,
you will give sighs
your slow cadence
and, as in a dance,
we will chase the black
where the moon fades ...
You will turn on the lights
of my dark mystery
and my weakness
it will be your madness,
and your intensity
it will be my magic.
And when time, slow,
it will become a hurricane
and the wind of the hands
will take us far,
I will untie my hair
as if it were a game
and you will wrap me up
until morning comes ...

IT WILL END

Will end
Your scent
in the room.
will end
the sound
of your guitar.
One night
a life…
Madness.

❖ ❖ ❖

UNTIL TOMORROW

I painted the soul
with your colors,
with your light
that I can't resist.
Who are you to burn
so my eyes?
Keep me with you
until tomorrow
until the morning
I will never stop your hand.
Burn my skin
with your breath,
my thoughts are fire.
Here, dawn already appears
the charm is reflected in the sea
and today is already tomorrow ...

JUSTICE

Oh justice
how many of tears
in this valley
must be paid
so that you
may reign
sovereign
on humanity?

◆ ◆ ◆

HAILSTORM

Grains
from the sky suddenly
black coffee in the path ...
Gentle tinnitus
disperses slowly
in the heart
its noise.

WATCH ME

Let me lie down next to you,
in a boundless meadow
under the moonlight.
Leave me lying
on the sand of your desire,
leave me there in the wind of your kisses.

Let me dissolve free
in the tight fist of your heart,
because I can't live
like a bird that twirls and sings
without his partner,
I can't live the day
if you deny me your love.

Come, like an angel
be found on the way to fate,
together we go
to listen to the sea.

Come on, let's hold hands
the heart will find peace.
To the breathlessness of being
love is the only remedy.

Besides you, there is no other life in me:
don't make me dust already
give me your sap
no longer suffer from the heart
between dark and fog,
don't let me think
and say that everything is in vain.
Don't just give me a look
but look at me:
tomorrow, in the dawn of love

blessed are the eyes
who has been able to see pure.

❖ ❖ ❖

WAR

From distant skies
winds of war blow,
the storm is near.
Evil
looms over humanity
after years of peace,
again they will be men
against men,
again it will be paid
useless blood.
No more though
that of friends ...

❖ ❖ ❖

YOU LIVED

You picked up buds
by the roadside;
grainy pupils
black in the evening;
your hands have scratched
and the heart, tearing gorse from the brambles.
You swallowed eagerly
the air of your south,
drinking peach orchards
of pink veils,
targeting olive groves
long-standing powers,
blue prosthesis.
You have read for years
in the eyes of children,
you saw the thorns
cover yourself with green;
stolen from the stars
uncertain flares,

of infinite nights.
You saw the stones
blossom yellow,
climbed walls
bitter lime,
he slapped you
frozen of death.
You shouted into the void;
you sang in the sun
tearing apart sunsets;
you dreamed in the sea,
you ran in the wind
flying in the mountains,
cracking the clouds.
You played with everything
and even with nothing;
you won and you lost ...
you lived.

I SAID

I said that the soul is not worth more than the body, and I said that the body is not worth more than the soul, that nothing, not even God is for anyone bigger than his self. I listen and see God in every object, yet I don't understand God in the least, nor that there can be anyone more wonderful than myself...

I see God in the faces of men and women and in my face in the mirror. I find letters sent by God on the streets each signed with his name and I leave them where they are because I know that wherever I go others will come on time, always and forever....

DREAMS

Dreams

they intertwine in the wind of life

they sail on tired illusions

buried in oblivion ...

EVIL

slender
are the days of darkness
and the disaster of beings
awaits the flesh
exhausted by the echo
and from the stamp
of our ruins
that are reborn.
Like a man

waiting outside

is bad:

he sees, listens

it is the endless torment of life.

And this human madness

haunts us ...

Then

peace

naked she rests on life.

The pleas

they will sleep in the deserts,

gestures

off in the dust

and raise your arms

remained in midair.

From the defeat

escape the missing

now consoled.

◆ ◆ ◆

THE SEA

The swaying of the sea
reminds me of vain tears
the pink clouds
good memories.
The seagulls

with the latest breezes
rotate
they let themselves be carried away.
I'd like to dive
in those serene waters
and never come back.

◆ ◆ ◆

MY LOOK

I wish you would meet my gaze.
It is a look that reads you inside
penetrates to the heart
and warms it up,
fills it with bright light
like fire.
It is the intoxication of a moment,
the happiness of a moment
when you feel alive
and master of what surrounds you,
when emotions

awaken the skin,
they make every fiber of your being vibrate
and fill you with new heat ...

POSITIVE THINKING

Greet the morning with a smile
Every day meditate a little.
Don't allow your mood
To be sad and gray.

Be happy and enjoy the day
The world is waiting
Just you.

So many things you can do
Do not hide
Do not be shy.
This day
It is yours in every way.

Be optimist!!!

◆ ◆ ◆

THE MEMORY OF YOU

Above the valleys
of the mountains
beyond the sun
beyond the borders
sweet Luigia
you move deftly in immensity.
You left behind
troubles and pains that weigh
about our existence.
Now you can thrust yourself with a vigorous wing
towards bright and serene fields;
your thoughts, like larks,
they fly freely
to the morning sky.
One day we will all get where you are:
in a resonant port, where our soul
will be able to drink perfume and color,
where vessels sliding into the sea
open wide arms to hold glory
of a pure sky, where eternal heat quivers.
I give you these words

because I remember you
equal to the most beautiful fairy tales
both in the night and in the crowd
dance like a joyful bird in my heart.
The memory of you, rosy, enchanting,
it whirls around.
You look more and more like the immortal sun,
to the horizons of a landscape
inflamed by rays.
Angel full of gaiety, how far you are!
I see in the photograph in front of me
your black hair caressed by the waves
disheveled by the wind;
You are so beautiful and simple
that I can't hold back the tears
and your voice still speaks to me: pure and intact.
suddenly
then nothing else
nothing but your face, dear Luigia
then tiredness, indifference
and want to sleep
and I even miss the desire to smile.

◆ ◆ ◆

THE WIND

Like leaves in the wind it sometimes seems to us to be fragile
and insecure, ready to suffer the directions imposed by
fate. But like them we are not. Aware of our intelligence and
strength we must be, because we become leaves when we
bend to the will of events. So by closing our eyes and digging
into the ego cave we can see the river of knowledge. And when
we drink from this source we will learn what our life really is
and that it is important not to be afraid of the wind but that
we will only have to ride it and be part of it. Maybe then we
will be at peace with ourselves and feel strong and confident.
It is up to us to choose to be leaves or to become a men ...

IN THE SHORE

The sand
moved by the waves
and by men
and not,

who go to the washer.
Glimmers of sun
screams of desires
ambiguous laughter,
they are chasing each other
lightning
nell'arenile
now deserted.

❖ ❖ ❖

HOAX

A trap
endless
nothing but fantasies,
lost
the carefree cheerfulness
the most beautiful
of my days.

Alas!
I haven't forgotten
and I guard
a kind of pride
with which I caressed so much
your gaze
and lightning
filtered by your eye.

❖ ❖ ❖

INVOCATION

Listen
please
this voice
that comes up hovering
through the ways of heaven,
crying
the trouble of life
the scream of pain
that echoes
within the walls
of this gray valley.
Listen

please
my plea,
give me back a smile
that I have lost
when Luigia
passed away.

◆ ◆ ◆

THE LIGHT

It has already fallen in the evening
slow on everything
and the pain of the day rests.
Doves fly away
with their cautious flight
while I remain motionless.
A human cry disturbs my peace:
I feel it in the dark
call me and surround me
long and bitter.
But the solemn hour still strikes ...
Oh, how I would like to come to light!
Every human power
it is an infinite evil
and the cry of life
hides behind, in the dark.

Oh, blissful trip
in the solitude of light!
How long will you keep waiting!?

❖ ❖ ❖

MY CITY

It rains on the city
all sad and gray,
the horizon is cloudy
and I as I wish
know how to fly!
Like birds …
Street from the earth
to heaven
where there is eternal feast
that reigns always shines
where every soul
can quench their thirst
of the most forbidden secrets,
while heady scents
go slowly
to cloud my mind.

❖ ❖ ❖

THE DEATH

Death is nothing.
Does not matter.
I only went to the next room.
Nothing happened.
Everything remains exactly as it was.
I am me and you are you and past life
that we lived so well together
it is unchanged, intact.
What we have been for each other,
we still are.
Call me by my old name ...
Talk about me with the ease you have always used
Don't change the tone of your voice.
Do not take a forced air of solemnity or pain.
Laugh like we always laughed.
Smile, think of me and pray for me.
Let my name remain forever
That familiar word that was.

◆ ◆ ◆

OUR SOUL

Our soul
naked she shows herself,
freeing the eyes
forbidden desires.
Masks drop
discovering the truest part,
letting it fly away
along with the whispered words,
the moment of silence
in which I captured
your gaze.
I am unarmed,
in hands
just the courage to want you,
the unconsciousness of letting go.
The time of sighs
hasn't come yet,
the flesh waits silently.
In the peace of the night
we deceive time,
dream of the heart
in the first rays of dawn ...

PEACE

Peace is within me.
The peace that extinguishes
invades me;
the strength is dozing ...
and vanishes.
goes out in me
the will
gently
but inevitably
I abandon myself
to this silence
so unnatural.

THE PASSION

You appeared like the evening
when the twilight

covers our slender bodies
with a mantle of tender light.

You surprised me
behind
then making parade before my eyes
your quilted cloak of stars;
you spread it under these humble feet
and the song of its planets
he prayed to me in silence
to walk over the Milky Way,
so that sweetness arose
from the caresses of my steps.

The universe has woven
our lives
like stringy gold braids
and while we were sailing
from one star to another
from one bank to another,
we surrendered to mutual beauty
that flowed from our essences,
like thousands of colorful fountains
ready to reach the breath of the cosmos
through the union of our bodies.

And that's how you appeared to me
giving moments that are not moments,
eyes that didn't belong to you

hands that weren't yours,
but the attributes of the universe
who focused on your whole being,
and they made me travel
within the dimension of desire,
creating in me a new and more subtle reality.
Passion.

◆ ◆ ◆

YOUR IMAGE

Your image
is present:
clean, transparent
similar to the sea
untouched.
The beach is deserted
the cold air,
My heart
full of intense emotions,
like the blue of the sky.
Romantic landscape!

Yet nothing calm
my restless soul
that breaks
violent as the waves.

THE LOVE OF THE NIGHT

The love of the night
will wake us up in the morning
with the desire for our smile.
The sun will not erase
the passion that the moon
he gave us.
It was unique to get rid of all the masks
and love us with such intensity!
In the beauty of your eyes
I lived an infinite passion,
in an instant I felt a whole life.
We experienced this immensity,
we will remember our senses,
we will remember everything about us.
The moon made us splendid lovers,

accomplices in the night of a brief treasure,
that will remain ours alone.

◆ ◆ ◆

THE ABSENCE OF YOU

The absence of you
make me invade
even in dreams,
and it's gorgeous.
I dream fresh sheets,
our naked bodies,
one inside the other,
the pleasure that multiplies
and expands
making nothing and insignificant
everything else.
My body
it is pervaded by impetuous waves
of the stormy sea,
the dark and clear sky
illuminated by thunderbolts,
wet beach
wet by fierce impetus
of the icy waters ...

I look at your mouth
and I wish to gently touch it,
I look at your smile,
I listen to your voice
and I would like to whisper "I want you".
Pure emotions, real sighs,
alchemy of feelings …
Only you can pass this on to me,
only to you could I give myself completely.

◆ ◆ ◆

THE MIRROR

My mind was a mirror.
He saw what he saw, he knew what he knew.

In my youth my mind was like the mirror of a fast-moving car, which captures and immediately scatters the features of the landscape. Then in time, deep scratches were produced on the mirror, between which the outside world crept in, and my most secret self emerged. This is the birth of the soul in pain, a birth made of gains and losses. The mind sees the world as a separate thing, and the soul makes it one with itself. A scratched mirror does not reflect images, this is the silence of wisdom.

◆ ◆ ◆

MELANCHOLY

How far they are
all the candors
and the rejoicing of reality!
Towards a spring of remorse
who have fled
the black winters of my boredom
and disgust
and sadness!
And now here I am alone
melancholic and lonely
Tetra

and more icy than an ancestor.
interweave
in the middle of the green branches
my thoughts
that slowly wander in the night.

SEA

We were there.
We looked far
beyond the green of the branches,
beyond sunset,
beyond the night
which slowly fades.

Welcome our words in the waves
you plunge dreams into the abyss
and illusions,
flood this story,
don't make me remember
the scent of thoughts,
ambiguous caresses
my love song.

Fly my infinite weakness ...

I stop to listen
the song of the sirens,
I consume that magical encounter,
my lost reason
find peace,
in your hands ...

Dawn tinges with silver
the new day.

MOMENTS OF GLORY

It's the end
of a dream
of eternal glory

cradled for years.
It's the end
and I don't have it
the other side,
not even the medal.
Nor of life
nor of glory
I have full hands.
Ah, glory!
What deception!

MUSIC

Puppet
in the threads of music

it's me,
and in the pentagram of life
I let myself be carried away
and vaulting relentlessly
until its sweet drop ...

◆ ◆ ◆

IN THE WOOD

I walk with my eyes to heaven
thinking about life.
All around desert ...
There is silence.
A thin ray of sunshine
that filters from the branches
peeps.
The sweet quiet
that reigns supreme

in these meadows it is so far!
The crying goes so far as to touch my heart.
eternal confusion
lie upon us miserable,
There is no love
of joy.
Oh justice!
Descend finally
on this world of sins!

◆ ◆ ◆

IN MY MIND

In my mind
you have the splendor of a rosy dream,
but your lip quivering
lets me see a burning desire
to find a place in my reality.

My sweet friend,
very pure diamond
clear look of shining water
How long will I have to stay away?

Until the moment
on a bright morning

our bodies will join
in an eternal instant
merging into the ecstasy of passion
forgetful of every identity.

Here, the wind is also silent ...

DEPARTURE

Once again
the weather
will transform
the emptiness left
will materialize

It will take shape
it will become concrete
in the removal
in separation
in detachment

It will make you weigh
its passing
slow

and will make them conflicting
moods

It will
competing
memories
feelings
emotions

As long as there is a return
that he will find
a more mature affection.

◆ ◆ ◆

THOUGHTS

By now
we no longer know anything
we have lost our memory.

The good, the bad ...
unusual vision
that disturbs and riots
the horizon of my mind.
Then
we find ourselves wandering
sad and lonely children
in a note of languor
and eternal quiet,
and we just have to sleep,
to sleep
to dream...

◆ ◆ ◆

THOUGHTS (to Mirko)

You are like the wind,

the rain,

the sun, which makes my soul blossom

in spring.

I look at your eyes

and I love you more than my life ...

Do you want to marry me?

THOUGHTS

Love is finding one's soul through the soul of the beloved.
When the loved one withdraws from your
soul, then you have lost his soul.

It is written: I have a friend, but my pain has no friends.

I remember the dew of my eyes that penetrated, like a
thought that slips into the heart of a flower. I remember
the long years of solitude, in my home, in an attempt to get
back and change my pain into higher consciousness. But
there were all my pains, sitting next to me, an image that
ended up entering my heart, bringing you infinite peace.

Even in the deepest sleep I think of the torment of life. So to a contrasted love, or a frustrated ambition, or an error that has upset my existence, irreparably, to the last pain. They will arise in the dreams of our last sleep, until full liberation from the celestial sphere reaches you, like awakened, healed and cheerful eyes in the morning. You should be completely dead when you are half dead, and not mock life, nor cheat love ...

I have observed my face in the mirror many times: a ship at anchor, with the sail lowered. In reality it does not represent my landing place but my life. Because love was offered to me but I refused its enticements; pain knocked on my door, but I was afraid; ambition called me but I feared the risks. Still, I longed to make sense of my life. Now I know it is necessary to raise the sails and be carried by the winds of fate, wherever they push the ship. Giving meaning to life can lead to madness, a meaningless life is the torture of restlessness and vague desire: it is a ship that ardently seeks the sea but is afraid ...

FOR YOU

For you
I will let myself be carried away by the wind,
I will listen to the melody of the seagulls,
light as a feather
I'll join you,
sailing between the oceans.

I will touch the stars,
I will feed on light,
between magical auroras.
I will come to you
to kiss you endlessly.

I will be reborn from your mouth,
I will become a dream
I will ride the wings of fantasy,
caressed by the sun
and cradled by clouds ...
in this reality
now full of your presence.

Sweet is your thought
when it reaches mine
merging into one.

❖ ❖ ❖

MEMORIES

I look at the horizon,
taste the taste of memories
that caress my memory ...

My heart in prison
it makes my mind free
to trespass in the essence of tender looks,
and the sky is only a large opaque blanket
that warms anger.

The desire to escape
from the oppressed feeling that made me up,
makes me want to rape my eyes ...
Yes, my eyes ...
than with their tender gaze
they draw your body by my side.

A small room,
too small, for such a great passion.
My breath condenses on every wall
making the stone tear, cold and freezing.
I feel the euphoria for a simple word,
that unleashes an ocean of emotions in me .....

This is too big to be conceived by everyone.

I RUN AFTER THE WIND

I chase the wind

so as not to miss
not even a breath,

hoping he touched you

bringing me something about you.

Whenever I look at the sky
I see them, your eyes.

All the rest
they are only darkness.

You brought me
in your fantasy world.

Welcome ... love!

PORTRAIT

Always inevitably
my gaze stops on your portrait,
on your photograph
on your face scratched by the wind
pervaded by occult images,
enigmas of your being a woman.
Shadow dances
your mild eyes furrow
cadencing nenie of pierced illusions,

today to love thorns in the heart.
It emerges, from these soft colors,
the melancholy breath
emerging from heavy sighs
that mow the soul,
and awaken lost thrills.
Time burns goals
and how to corroded ruin
existence lies down
in the shadow of a dark decline,
and hover over your face
the fleeting yearning for youth gone.
Always inevitably
my gaze stops on your portrait
on your photograph
I mirror myself in your feelings
capturing palpable emotions
of parallel symbiosis,
we both receive the echo of memories
that like the sea is never silent.

WISDOM

A great black sleep
falls on my life:
my hopes
you sleep
sleep desires.
Melancholic story!
Heaven is upon us
calm and blue,
a nearby tree
swing his palm,
a bird
sings his lament.
Life is here
simple and quiet
and like a whisper
my bitter thoughts

with restless and crazy flight
they hover over the ocean
macerating in itself the memories ...

LOVE

I wanted to believe
in love,
and now the despair
Is again
In me....

I HEAR

I feel, how it happened to me. I feel, like when I realized I reached you, like when your voice told me to love me, like when love forced me to know, I feel ... and while I look at your eyes inevitably alive ... If there was a way to I would describe love, but the only thing I can do while I look at you is getting lost in everything you represent to me ...

SUFFERING

Don't ask yourself anything
at the moment
maiden of hope,
answer only
will have to end
one day
all of this.

❖ ❖ ❖

DREAMS

Slow kisses
on the shore of an impassive sea.
Bluish horizons
stretch the vast arms
to tighten the glory
of pure love.
Among the caresses,
naked with water
you swim...
and from my wound
beautiful,
you drank
coral whispers,
until the cry
of sun and tides
braided between the legs

LONELINESS

Loneliness
in the heart
like mist envelops
smothers
the arid limbs,
while ardent music
they travel slowly
the path
of memories.

STARS

The stars...
I get lost
in the middle of the night
without cold
nor pain,
I don't feel anything anymore
and slowly
I abandon myself
to a sleep
that has no awakening.

AND I WAIT FOR YOU....

Enveloping desire for you....

Kiss my mouth
play with the warmth of your hands
let yourself be guided by instinct
which has the flavor of the soul.

I wait for your whisper
you caress me lightly,
that impregnate me with you
for an infinite moment,
like that day, when
you stole my soul
ruining my heart
staying in it.

How many times

I'd like to know where your thought leads ...
If he takes mine by the hand
if it follows the paths of my body ...

Unlimited desires
entwine my flesh.

scrolls
frosty and limited time
and I'm waiting for you ...

◆ ◆ ◆

ALL MY DEMONS

I'm here
with all my demons.
Your image
is present:

clean, transparent
similar to the sea
untouched.

My breath
it condenses
on every wall
making the room water,
cold and freezing.

My heart
full of intense emotions.
Nothing calm
the restless soul
that breaks
violent,
like the waves
of the stormy sea.

Close my eyes,
that I can know
in this long wait,
the path of your fantasy.
Abandon yourself to oblivion,
where the senses can feed
of thrills and words
to fly to the wind.

I stay here

with all my demons,
but one
what I would like,
the only one I can't have ...

❖ ❖ ❖

I WANT TO HEAR YOU TELL YOU ARE MINE

Want you, your voice
Which is sweet melody for my soul.
Volgia of a thousand kisses
Feel like your hands on my body
To go crazy with your caresses.
Want to give myself to you madly
Because you can say YES to love ...
My lips are looking for yours
To breathe together ...
I explore your back with my fingers
I want you to groan in madness
I want to be told ... "you are mine ..."
Drink from my cup
Quench your thirst

Make me jump and moan
Wrap my body
Let me lose in a maze of pleasure ...

◆ ◆ ◆

I WOULD LIKE TO BE

I would like to be clear that,
on summer mornings,
enter your room dimly,
offering to your awakening
the greeting of the new day.

I wish I was
the air you breathe
to be able to follow closely
your gaze,
and to know
the world around you.

I wish I was
one of those trivial things
that you use frequently
in order to be part,
in this simple way
of your days.

I wish I was ...

I would like to be the woman you love
like you've never loved
none before.

So, for a moment
let me imagine it.
Let me take refuge
inside the pillow
that every night
welcome your breaths
and share your dreams
more hidden.

Having you so close
I would have a chance
to hold in my hands
your face,
caress it slowly,
and donate to your lips
a kiss.

Then how would you do it
a sudden breath of wind
that for a moment he touched your hair
I would whisper sweetly to you
"My love, I love you..."

I WOULD LIKE TO TALK TO YOU ABOUT LOVE

I listen to your voice without hearing the words.

I feel your breath without feeling its breath, I
have you without you being there.

Follow your arms, touch your mouth, be touched
by you and all the rest is in vain. I only wait for
your hands to abandon myself to love ...

Since I came into the world, I have always had with me a heavy
suitcase held together by ropes of courage and desire to live.
Time and experiences made it heavier, swelled it, blew the
locks. Then I needed new ropes of courage and stronger hands
to drag it; stronger hands to drag it against the wind that slows
down your pace and draws wrinkles on your face, against the
fear that takes refuge in your heart and makes it burst ... until
at a certain point you fly away with Love, without a suitcase!

I would like to fly away, together with you, free from
doubts and fears, join our bodies in a single dance,
let us discover lovers only from the night ...

Listen to the music that sings in me, it's a tender symphony played by my heart that jumps every time I look at you ...

I would like to talk to you about love with laughing eyes, I would like to introduce you to the beating of my lips, the movement of my soul, the passion that infiltrates and is lost between my senses. I would like you to hear the flow of my blood, the deafening voices hovering over my sleep. I would like you to hear the melody of my orgasm ...

Listen to our story made of words and emotions ... one of those stories that are not forgotten, one of those stories whose words are canceled by the wind but whose emotions remain tattooed in the soul.

And my soul is that of a gazelle: like her, in fact, she is free to run in the grasslands of the senses, for eternity ...

THAT DAY CAME
That day came and I saw the sun,
then came the evening
and I saw the sun of that day
reflected in your eyes,

I felt the waters of the river flow
and then the music
that accompanied your voice
and you who let yourself be carried away
from its melody.
I watched your movement
and I was immediately captured
from sweet and strange fantasies.
Desire as if by magic came true:
not the fire, but your warm lips,
not the fire but the crackle of whispers
of your eyes lit ...

Thinking of you
my heart opens
and like a torment,
the memory of your face haunts me.
Like wound flaps
that bleeds blood, always blood,
your thought is present.
I tried to close
the rooms of my heart,
but your memory chases me ...

I see you again, walk,
and walk with your pink feet
on the sand of my heart.
Impetuous sinking
your naked flowers scattering everywhere,
without escape, the petals of passion.

You are like the wind that fled the sea,
to perfume the rooms of my soul,
you are like the tide going
and nobody will ever stop,
you are like a seagull held prisoner
who desperately seeks freedom ...

I just think about you,
I am lost in intense desire
to dive into a whirlwind of passion
to land on the island of love,
where I feel shipwrecked in my own land.
And so, immersed in this sea,
which is our life,
I would see the reflected light of your face
(your face is a star, which you let me capture),
while segments of heaven
enchant my gaze
which opens up to free and penetrable spaces.
For me, that memory
is your gaze
on this cold day,
and in my living so absurd
you are the port
of a long walk in the ocean,
where I now rest.
Through thick bushes
I will hurt my soul
chasing your tracks,

and I marked on the heart
every emotion that has become poetry.
I colored my soul
with your light
that I can't resist.
Who are you to burn my eyes like this?
Come to my dreams slowly
and take the love that's in me.
I didn't wait for you,
silently take me
and I will not look up;
Together
we will take off

towards a sea of pleasure

and we will abandon ourselves to the waves of sleep,

that fill the eyelids

of the music of the stars,
impetuous and very sweet

that comes from beyond infinity.

I'd like to sleep on your chest

and wake up with you next,

I wish I always had you ...

This is love, life,

the mirror of the waters,

the hiss of the wind that accompanies your voice,

this is the magical eternal mystery of love ...

◆ ◆ ◆

I WOULD LIKE TO FIND

I would like to find a distant land
in which it can be insinuated
my wild and lost heart.
I would like to find a single moment,
an intense and fleeting moment
in which to live
the perception of your body.
I would like to take you strongly
with poignant impetus
of those who crave a bold desire....

I would like to untie this knot
that rises slowly to the throat
until you breathe ...

ACKNOWLEDGEMENT

Thanks to everyone who shared
special moments with me.

ABOUT THE AUTHOR

Barbara Castelnuovo

Barbara Castelnuovo was born in Busto Arsizio on January 14, 1975. Having moved to Sicily from her native Lombardy for a few years, she reserves, demonstrating her training path, the widest spaces of memory to the suggestive country visions, to mountain landscapes, to clear skies, to feelings typical of childhood and adolescence, whose re-enactment constitutes a constant, almost exclusive object of its inspiration. This collection represents an inner journey characterized by a succession of emotions and moods, from pain to love, from frustration to passion ... up to the discovery of a new dimension and awareness:

Only those who love know. Only those who know how to go beyond the limits of rationalization and follow their instincts by running through the grasslands of the senses ... Only those who love are alive. Poor who does not love!

Printed in Great Britain
by Amazon